Squeak

Vera Valentine

SQUEAK

VERA VALENTINE

Copyright © 2022 Word Chick Content, LLC | All Rights Reserved

The characters and events portrayed in this book are fictitious. Any similarity to real persons, living or dead, is coincidental and not intended by the authors.

No part of this book may be reproduced, or stored in a retrieval system, or transmitted in any form by any means electronic, mechanical, photocopying, recording, or otherwise, without express written permission of the publisher or authors, except as permitted by U.S. copyright law.

ISBN: 9798385852956

LEGAL INFO

An Unfortunately-Necessary Warning: If you have received or downloaded an ebook version of this book from a source OTHER than:

- The Kindle Unlimited program,
- A direct purchase from Amazon under the ASIN ending in LGN, or
- An ARC or promotional copy provided directly from or certified by the author (Vera Valentine) via Bookfunnel,

you are reading a FRAUDULENT COPY, are committing THEFT, and are SUPPORTING PIRACY. Sources of income derived from pirated books often come from overseas sites that launder or provide money to terrorist organizations, human trafficking, and other illegal activities.

In addition, you are consciously damaging our ability to earn a living as authors, as this doesn't simply prevent us from getting paid for our work, it jeopardizes our ability to sell our books on Amazon. Please don't steal, promote stealing, or download pirated books - most authors are more than happy to hook you up with a copy in exchange for a simple review. We do our best to be good people - please meet us where we stand. Thanks, and sorry to get heavy about it - we really do love and appreciate our legitimate readers.

Now, onto the good stuff!

To the one and only Beatrix Hollow, my monstersmut frand and the grumpy to my sunshine. You did this, hope you're happy with yourself.

To Clio Evans and Ashley Bennett, who didn't stop this from happening either, although they had several chances to. You're also to blame.

I love y'all.

A NOTE FROM THE AUTHOR

A dedicated art student at her local community college, Poppy practically lives inside her sketchbook. Drawn to the distracted crowds of the local zoo, her planned day of anonymous figure-sketching is interrupted by the charming Sebastian - and his brooding, borderline-rude friend Keane. Little does she know the two have a twisted secret that defies imagination - and the pressure on both of them is increasing by the day. As an intricate plan takes shape to secure their freedom, the twists and turns they face - and a pair of very intriguing knots - might just unwittingly tie Poppy to both of them, forever.

Squeak is a **balloon animal shifter omegaverse novella** with (artistic takes on) OV designations and omegaverse-specific concepts like knotting, heats, ruts, nests, mate bites, bondings, and more. There is a brief (non-main-character) death at the very end. There is discussion of past violence and sexual compulsion/slavery, but it's all occurred by the time the story starts. If I've missed mentioning any content considerations you feel should be in this list, please let me know! The safety and comfort of my readers always takes precedence.

POPPY

It wasn't the heat, it was the sunny glare in my eyes that drove me to seek out shade. The zoo was, predictably, crowded for a weekend but that worked just fine for me - unlike most of the people here, I was watching the visitors, not the animals. An annoying prickling sweat was starting under the straps of my backpack, which I shrugged off, letting the barely-there breeze slide across my damp t-shirt.

After a few claustrophobic minutes, I cut through the meandering crowd to my favorite destination: a wide, low wall outside the tortoise enclosure. Situated kitty-corner to a busy intersection of foot paths, it was the ideal place to perch for people-watching and sketching. I plunked down cross-legged, wordlessly claiming the space, and unzipped my backpack to retrieve my sketchbook and pencil case.

Taking a deep, slow breath, I lost myself in tracing vague shapes to build on, enjoying the soft sensation of repetition, graphite on smooth paper. Every few minutes, I took some quick glances at my unwitting models as they oohed and ahhed over the marmosets.

An hour later, I'd managed to sketch out a family with an adorably precocious little girl in pigtails and a striking older gentleman resting on his cane. I set my pencil down, my eyes aching from squinting, and my throat painfully dry. Even in the shade, the early May heat was just oppressive enough to notice on a prolonged outing and the fine hair at my temples was already plastered to my skin. Patting the side of my backpack for the looped top of my water bottle, I sighed. My full travel bottle was still sitting on the kitchen counter, waiting patiently to be slid into that empty side pocket. *Of course.*

Glancing between the restroom water fountain across the way and down to my belongings, I frowned. I really didn't want to pack it all up just to trek across the crossroad area for a few seconds. I was just scanning the crowd and weighing the risk of a quick trip when a smooth male voice cut through the murmur of the crowd.

"Hey, Red!" I squeezed my eyes closed, straightening my shoulders from where they'd instinctively hunched. Oh good, some asshole that was going to hit on me and struggle to take no for an answer. Christ, even the frigging zoo wasn't safe.

My fire engine red-dyed hair wasn't meant to make me a wallflower, obviously, but I hadn't realized it would make me a beacon for douchecanoes, too. College, at least walking the campus between classes, had become nearly unbearable with the sheer number of thirsty interactions. I plastered on my best 'thanks but no thanks' smile and queued a hasty excuse to leave on my tongue as I looked up.

The soft thomp-thomp sound of balloons gently bouncing off one another greeted me, the inflatables in question hovering over a dazzling smile. I swallowed that hasty excuse down my dry throat like a stubborn pill when I saw the man holding them.

The epitome of tall, dark, and handsome standing in front of me managed a hotness quotient that overrode the corny old-timey red-and-white striped vest he wore. The zoo had been trying out a vintage aesthetic for their vendors this year. What had looked cheap and gimmicky on everyone else I'd seen made *him* stunningly attractive, from his glossy black curls to his impeccably-polished shoes of the same hue. A gleaming gold name tag proclaimed him *Sebastian* in block lettering.

"Hey, sorry. I didn't know your name." His smile grew a little shy. "I wanted to let you know I'd keep an eye on your things if you had to use the bathroom. I'm just standing out here anyway."

"The...what?" Flustered now, I blinked at him, looking in the direction he'd tilted his head. "Oh! Uh, yeah, thanks, but I actually just wanted to get a drink of water."

Sebastian wrinkled his nose. "Damn. Sorry to be the bearer of bad news, then. The fountain's busted, some kid tried to stand on it yesterday and broke the spout. Could I get you a bottle of water instead? You look warm."

I shook my head, turning to reach for my bag and sketchbook again. A light breeze took some of the edge off the heat, the soft, hollow sound of rustling balloons telling me Sebastian hadn't walked away. I was oddly pleased he hadn't.

"I'd probably get in trouble if you had a heat stroke, you know. Could lose my job." His tone was teasing, and I smirked as I zipped up my bag.

"Sounds like you were on thin ice to begin with then, *Sebastian*." I teased back, shouldering my backpack and turning to find him grinning at me.

"Maybe I'm on thin ice for giving out so many free balloons to kids, *Red*. Ever think of that?" He tugged the fistful of balloon ribbons in his grasp with a dramatic faux-forlorn expression and a lofty sigh. "If I got fired, it'd sure break a lot of little hearts."

I rolled my eyes at the ploy but shrugged good-naturedly. I *was* thirsty, no sense being an idiot about it. What was he going to do, murder me in broad daylight? "Okay, fine. Can't have you losing your job because I keeled over, I guess."

"Well, I'm glad I'm preferable to sun stroke." He laughed and rolled his eyes. "The guy at the snack bar owes me a favor and it's time for my break. Join me?"

I shuffled my backpack on my shoulder again, stomach tightening pleasantly at the sight of my unexpected companion's deep brown eyes. Before I caught myself and looked away, I straight-up stared at his amazing, feathery lashes. They were the unfair sort they sold at cosmetics counters, and this bastard was out here flaunting them like some kind of influencer.

"Oh, sure. Lead on. I'm Poppy, by the way."

"Pleasure to meet you, Poppy. What brings you to the zoo? I don't think I've seen you here before." Sebastian tied off his fistful of balloon strings on a slender looped post beside the bathroom building, nodding towards a tree-shaded path.

"Figure drawing." I tugged my backpack strap and tilted my head towards it. "I have to check off a couple of boxes for my classes in terms of models, and I don't like cooping myself up in a classroom. Makes me feel like...yanno." I raised a brow at the monkey cages as we passed them.

Sebastian hummed his agreement, pace growing leisurely as we approached the long, well-shaded bridge that spanned the maned wolf enclosure. The musk wafting up from the ground below us made me wrinkle my nose; this was one of the less-pleasant realities of the zoo on a hot day. "How about you? Worked for the zoo very long? I came pretty frequently last year when I was sketching animals and I don't remember seeing you."

He shrugged lightly. "Yeah. My friend and I were traveling with a circus for a long time and there was - well, we didn't get along well with management, let's put it that way. Once we struck off on our own, we found out this place was hiring, and our carnie skills translated pretty well. So, here we are, melting in the heat right alongside you."

"We? Oh, you mean your friend in concessions?" I shifted uncomfortably, prickly sweat tickling along my spine. I just knew my hair was probably frizzed beyond recognition, and what little makeup I'd put on that morning probably looked awful. But hey, Sebastian was still being flirty with me, right? Maybe it wasn't that bad. Speaking of, why did his curls look so good? It would be weird to ask a guy for conditioner recommendations, right? Between those eyelashes and his unfairly frizz-less hair, this guy was seriously wrecking the curve, though.

He nodded, eyes searching for something up ahead. "Mhm. Keane's got an attitude problem but he's really sweet once you get to know him. Don't mind him if he's a little snippy - he doesn't like the heat. Honestly, I don't either, but I deal with it a lot better than he does. That's why I take balloon duty and let him hang out in the booth. But hey - at least there's air conditioning in there, right? I'll smuggle you in the back so you can cool off too."

KEANE

I startled, chin nearly dropping out of my hand when the back door banged open - that was definitely Sebastian. He'd never quite managed to get the hang of doors after so many years of tent flaps and beaded curtains. I clapped the heavy dictionary-thick book I'd been reading closed, just in case a manager was with him, hurriedly dusting off the tiny burgundy flakes of dry leather that shed from the cracked spine. True, we'd gotten lucky with the sigils once, but we'd never managed to recreate that luck, and now time was running out. That meant I spent every spare moment I had researching, trying to tilt the scales in our favor. Tulpas weren't meant to rule the magics of their masters, and our borrowed power was starting to wane - the threads of the spell had worn dangerously thin. I slipped the book under the counter and frowned when a bright red head of hair ducked into the trailer after Sebastian, rather than our manager Angela's familiar dishwater blonde.

"Seb, who the fuck is this?" If I sounded annoyed, it was because I *was* annoyed. The interloper smiled and gave an awkward little finger-wave, cheeks flushed from the heat. My eyes snagged on the steel-blue of her own for a moment before they darted back to Sebastian, demanding an explanation. He knew damn well I was already on edge, I didn't need surprises.

He scowled in return and gave me a *look*. "This is Poppy, Keane. Poppy, this is the ill-mannered friend I evidently spoke too highly of. Keane, chill. I promised her a bottle of water because it's hot outside, that's all." He reached into the cooler and grabbed one of the water bottles, opening it and passing it to her.

"Poppy's an art student. She was sketching in the sun and the fountain was broken." Sebastian continued, raising an eyebrow at me as the girl drank. I knew what he was getting at - the sigils, if we could even find the right ones before the spell collapsed, would need an artist's hand. Beyond the actual intricacy required to make them, we were created beings, and couldn't manifest the intention they needed the way something *truly* living could. It'd be a little like trying to give a car a soul - the two halves were inherently incompatible.

Speaking of incompatible, I wasn't a fan of the way the redhead was currently eyeing my boyfriend. Sebastian was flirtatious, mainly because he was made to be the showman of the two of us, while I was the more stoic manifestation. My job had always been to get things done - set up the quarter poles, strike down the tent, pack up the wagon. Sebastian, meanwhile, had been the one to coax money from passersby for midway games, or tarot card readings from the Amazing Zina, our creator, tormentor, and former captor. What Seb and I now shared had been our first choice as free beings, and I'd be damned if I'd let anything come between us now. We'd worked too hard for it.

"Well, mission accomplished. Nice to meet you Poppy, but I

need to get back to work. Seb, I need to talk to you about... scheduling." It came out more brusque than I intended, and Poppy's smile faded, a worried crease forming between her brows. Of everything that had happened since we'd escaped Zina, the only thing I was truly afraid of now was losing Seb, and I didn't need some woman complicating everything, artist or no. If her feelings were bruised, so be it - she was a stranger to us and I wanted her gone. I wasn't lying, either: I *did* have work to do, it just wasn't concessions-related.

Seb was definitely angry with me, but escorted Poppy back through the narrow trailer out the back door without argument. I heard his faint apologies to her before he stomped back up the gridwork steps, alone. Some of the tension in my shoulders slid away now that she was gone, at least until he spoke up again.

He propped a hip against the cooler, grabbing a bottle and twisting the cap off sharply before taking a swig, glaring at me. "Keane. You were a complete asshole to that girl, and she didn't deserve any of it. She might have been able to *help* us. What the hell's gotten into you?"

"Me? What the hell's gotten into *you*, Seb? We're fighting for our lives and you're out - what, flirting with some girl? It's bad enough you insist we keep up this work nonsense, it's cutting into my research time and our protection is going to collapse any day now." I ground my teeth, willing away fearful visions of being back in Zina's trailer. I stormed past him, *this* trailer beginning to feel claustrophobic like *that* one had.

Seb palmed my shoulder, spinning me around and pinning me against the tall storage cubby doors. His voice was softer, injured. "Keane. You can't possibly think-"

I squeezed my eyes closed when hot tears threatened to escape, tensing my jaw as my throat thickened with emotion. "Think what? That you'll turn tail for a pretty face, a softer touch, now that we're free? Now that I'm not the only choice besides - besides *her,* Seb?

Zina had created us to serve her - there was no kinder way to phrase it. At first, when we were new to creation and exploring existence as men, it had been interesting. We'd been brought into being with all the sense of adult humans, but none of the actual experience. Obtaining that experience became a sort of game, a new task to learn. If we did well, she allowed us to remain in our new forms for longer periods of time. The problem was that Zina tightly controlled what we could know and learn - so much so that the idea that we could *also* enjoy pleasure was a revelation. She used us with no warmth or consideration at all, leaving us exhausted, used, and unsatisfied after she'd gotten what she wanted.

Seb and I had been careful since that fateful night, a few weeks before our escape. Zina had been especially cruel to Seb, accusing him of purposely underperforming in *that* task, grabbing her robe and storming out of the trailer. When she wanted us to service her sexually, our men's bodies would grow cocks - thick, long, and sporting an extra addition we hadn't realized wasn't normal until we spotted one of the roustabouts urinating against a wall one day. Conversely, when Zina was finished using our bodies in bed, we went as smooth between the legs as the plastic dolls carnival attendees won at toss-games.

I'd only meant to comfort Seb that night. He'd been crying from the pinches, slaps, and cruel names Zina always tormented him with during the act. Seb was easier to bring to tears, and seemed to suffer more, which was why she used him so often despite my pleas to use me instead. She only ever took one of us to bed at a time, forcing the other to stay in the next room. He'd been curled up in her bed, sniffling with each new bruise his fingertips found, throwing terrified, defeated glances at the door.

I simply joined him in bed, hugging him tight and turning him into my chest to cry it out.

There had been no real word for what Seb and I were to each other - not brothers, even though we'd been created at the same time, and far more than friends, though both prisoners. When his tear-stained lips met mine long moments later, desperately seeking comfort, we at least had a word for that: *lovers*. When our eager fumbling resulted in our very first pair of messy, writhing climaxes, something important shifted in both of us.

After that, one of us would stand lookout at the window while the other furtively searched through Zina's hidden cache of occult items. I eventually pieced together the reason Seb and I could maintain the entirety of our forms with one another: Zina's spell had made her the only *woman* with the ability to control us sexually. We guessed she hadn't considered a man could wield the spell, or didn't think we'd ever turn to one another like that. Either way, Seb and I counted the revelation as a blessing.

And after that first night together, we began to talk of dangerous things between stolen kisses - plans for life outside of Zina's grasp. We started to whisper more often, getting more bold about exploring one another in the process. One night, we weren't careful enough and lost track of time, waking up entangled to a furiously shrieking Zina. In a rage, she'd forced us out of our human forms and locked us in separate plastic boxes, the sides and tops studded with sharp, enchanted pins. It was sheer luck I'd already been preparing the sigils for our escape, and that the furious slam of the trailer door jarred the lid of my box enough that I could partially shift. I'd carefully wriggled free and opened Sebastian's box to free him too. Together, we painted our skin with sigils and walked, ran, and hitchhiked hundreds of miles away. When we felt we were far enough from our captor, we found work at the zoo to hopefully blend into society outside of the circus.

Zina had never spoken of her magic unless it was to threaten us into compliance, so we could only guess her initial intentions with tulpamancy. Both Sebastian and I had started creation as one of the most common sights under the tent or along the midway: colorful balloon animals. My dim first memories of consciousness were of bending and twisting, my maker's breath filling my body and pulling me through the dream world into this one. My next sensations were of Sebastian's nearness, and my very first understanding was that he was *like me*, and that made me *happy*. Until the night we escaped, that had been the first and last time I'd felt unguarded joy - the cruelty and threats had started shortly after.

Now, even with the stress of constant vigilance, Seb made me *happy*. He stood on his toes - I had a few inches of height on him - and kissed me softly. "No, Keane. Never. I told you when we left that nothing would ever separate us again. I meant it then and I meant it now - I'm just trying to help the only way I know how. Her linework is good from what I could see in her sketchbook, and she seems friendly. Luckily, even despite your shit attitude, she was still willing to talk to me after. She says she'll be visiting the zoo again soon, I can bring it up with her next time I see her."

I pulled him against my chest, tucking his head under my chin, jealousy striking like a serpent when I remembered the way she looked at what was *mine*. "No. Not her. We'll find another artist. In fact, *I* will."

Yes, that was a much better solution. I'd find an artist that wouldn't covet my lover, one we could trust, perhaps pay with some of the earnings we both had from our jobs. Being able to turn into balloon animals at will wasn't much of a superpower, all told, but it saved us a great deal on rent.

Seb squirmed a little in my embrace, and I knew an argument was on his tongue. Guilt rested heavily on my stomach as I deepened our embrace instead, silencing him with a sensual kiss and a slow exhalation of air. I felt the pressure against my thigh as that inflation found its way down the sympathetic path it knew so well, the bulge of Sebastian's knot wide and tempting beneath the thin striped cloth of his pants.

We were creations of air that didn't, strictly speaking, *need* to breathe, a particularly handy trait for what we'd discovered together those first few passionate nights. While I felt we'd perfected the act by sheer chance and repetition, apparently we weren't the first men to 'deep throat.' After Seb and I had first been hired on here, a smartphone from the lost and found offered an unexpected trove of lurid videos in a browser tab. We'd hungrily watched them all on a loop until the battery died, recreating them in the concessions trailer after hours.

"*Keane.*" Seb's admonishment came out breathy as I blindly reached out to the side, flicking the concessions sign from open to closed. I tugged down the shade down and latched it before dropping to my knees.

I made short work of his zipper and groaned as the heady scent of powdered sugar and latex sweetened the room. We were creatures of the carnival down to our cores, and Seb's arousal was a balmy night on the midway, a handful of bright balloons and the funnel-cake booth all colliding in the senses.

My tongue swept up the tempting bud of his balloon tie-knot, the playful little wrinkled ring that was quickly melting into his latex-wrapped cock. If I caught it before the shift completed, I got to take advantage of its hypersensitivity, and who could possibly turn *that* down?

Seb let out a high, birdlike cry, gracelessly falling back against the lid of another freezer as his legs shook. His fingers fisted in my hair, almost unconsciously, desperate for more. He was the most beautiful thing I'd ever seen when he came unraveled like this, his eyes closed and head tilted back in ecstasy. The pressure of his cock expanding in my mouth tickled my palate as he nudged and pushed himself deeper.

I knew I could tease him, drag him along the edge for hours if I wanted to, and the thought was tempting. But I only intended for this to be a distraction, not a marathon, and neither of us thought clearly if we didn't get a good night's sleep. Research time before the zoo opened was becoming a necessity, which meant late nights - even if I spent them having fun with Seb - needed to wait. I moved skilled fingers to the bulge near the base of his cock. This was our 'extra part' - one we'd ironically discovered was also called a knot.

I squeezed it lightly with my fingertips, forcing the bubble of air further up his shaft, then back down, just a few inches' worth of stroking. Seb whined and babbled, begging me not to stop, knuckles white and tensed where they gripped the freezer edge.

"Keane - please! Please, I'm so *close*- I ca- oh, *oh*!"

I palpated his knot rapidly, pumping his shaft with my other fist, twisting my grip fluidly as I moved up and down. The *thwhump* of air rapidly scurrying up his shaft, expanding its red latex-coated edges, sent his cockhead ballooning into a sphere on my tongue. His smaller tie-knot reappeared at the tip and I flicked it rapidly with my tongue as he panted, giving it a gentle tug with my teeth. Seb tossed his head back with a gasp, his end unknotting with a snap on my tongue before hot, thin jets of funnel cake icing flowed out to soothe the sting.

I sucked with a happy hum, reveling in the actual, literal sweetness of my balloon shifter lover. He always blushed so beautifully when I called him my favorite dessert, but it was the truth. The bone-deep sigh of satisfaction he gave afterwards was also my favorite sound, and I loved the way he always gave a few languid strokes in and out of my mouth, even after he'd finished. He'd shyly admitted recently that seeing me lick up and swallow what passed for our cum was a massive turn on for him, so naturally I worked that angle mercilessly.

As he reluctantly dragged himself from between my lips, the soft, slow hiss of Seb's deflating cock kissed the side of my neck with air. I smiled against his thigh, nuzzling it affectionately before standing back up. This was mine. *Seb* was mine. The sweetness still lingering in my mouth was *mine*.

Seb smiled lopsidedly, blissed out, and reached down to cup between my legs, pulling me into a kiss. His chest rose as he pulled in a deep breath, preparing to inflate me too, but I cut the kiss short with a gentle peck on his lips. He tilted his head with a quizzical expression, slowly exhaling the air he'd pulled for me with a raised brow.

"I'm fine, don't worry about that. I want to get a good night's rest so I'm fresh for research tomorrow. I don't need to be halfway through a page and have some early bird visitor banging on the window for popcorn." I smirked as Seb made a cute little noise of disappointment, pouting at me before giving a resigned nod. Distraction successful, I thought triumphantly. Hopefully he wouldn't even remember the girl's name tomorrow - Prissy, Polly, whatever it was. Her blue eyes were annoyingly easy to remember, but they'd fade just fine with time.

As we slid into one another's arms and let the shift take over; a single intricate twist of red and purple balloons taking the place of our human forms. We preferred to rest entwined like this, and had ever since we'd escaped, now that Zina couldn't force us apart any longer. Our joined balloon gently drifted down with a hollow, musical *thwonk* to settle on the freezer lid. I pushed the annoyingly intrusive memory of the girl's grey-blue gaze out of my mind as sleep claimed us both.

POPPY

After I'd gotten home and showered all the sweaty ick off, narrowly talking myself out of burning my sweat-drenched clothes, I flopped down in bed and actually got a full night's sleep for once. I woke to the bright sunlight of early afternoon rudely shining through my blinds and stumbled to the bathroom to do my wake-up routine. Freshly scrubbed and brushed, I sank back down on my bed with my sketchbook. After blindly groping for a pencil in my bag, I flipped to a blank page and lines and shadows flowed with more ease than they had in awhile. My artist's eye had gotten tangled in Sebastian's loose, silky curls during the short time we'd spent together, and my fingers itched to sketch them. Surprisingly, however, the eyes staring back up at me now weren't Sebastian's bright ones, but the suspicious, narrowed ones of the man from the concessions trailer - Keane. His "friend" that I suspected was either more than that, or else Sebastian was completely frigging clueless.

Sketched-Keane's angular jawline and dark eyes still flashed with anger at me as my pencil twitched, bringing him to life despite myself. Was he mad at me because I'd flirted with Sebastian a little? It wasn't like I'd done it in front of him, so what the hell was his problem? Maybe he was just irritated from the heat and took it badly - lord knows I'd been on the verge of feeling that way myself. I couldn't wait for fall.

Sighing when my memories failed to agree on what Keane's nose actually looked like, I closed my book with a huff. I hated this part of the process, the visual equivalent of writer's block. Could I sneak back to the zoo to get a good look at him without being a creeper? This sketch would work perfectly for my emotion assignment; Professor Ansen wanted us to find a "stern" model to work on this week. The kindly man with the cane and the exuberant little girl I'd created yesterday wouldn't do, and they were the wrong size anyway. Keane, meanwhile, had somehow commanded two hours of my time and an entire page while I zoned out and sketched. It'd be a shame to waste the work, even if he'd been kind of an asshole to me.

I tucked my sketchbook back in my bag, mind made up. I'd already cut it too close to my assignment deadlines the last two weeks; finding a new model by tomorrow would be a hassle. I'm sure Keane wouldn't be happy to see me again, which would work just fine for my needs. This time, when I left my water bottle behind on the counter, it was a deliberate move - one that made a smirk tug at my lips.

An unexpected jolt of nerves curled in my stomach and across my palms as I made the short trip to the zoo, moving to my spine as I walked in with a flash of my season pass. As I moved past my favorite spot on the tortoise enclosure wall, my heart sank a little - a bored-looking middle aged man was selling balloons where Sebastian had yesterday. I was hoping to add the attractive balloon-seller and his ridiculous eyelashes to my personal sketches after I'd finished Keane's, but it looked like that would have to wait.

Once the concession trailer came into view, my nerves kicked up again. Was this creepy? I didn't feel creepy sketching figures like the family or the older man, but this felt...personal. I straightened my shoulders and shook it off, reminding myself that it was a public place and it wasn't like I was drawing nude fan art of him. Would it be more or less awkward if he knew I was there? I decided that *I'd* feel less creepy making him aware of my presence, so I slipped into the short line to grab a bottle of water.

Even though I nervously ran through potential interactions in my head while I waited, I was still surprised at the vitriol in his eyes when Keane realized I'd returned.

"Can I help you?" The faint smile he plastered on looked dangerous, nearly unhinged, thanks to the complete lack of light in his eyes.

While I hadn't done anything truly stupid - felony-level stupid, anyway - in my life, no one could accuse me on not being impulsive at inopportune times. Sure, I could say that I asked because I needed to see the emotion clearly, but in reality, I bristled at his doubling down on dickishness and felt like poking a soft spot.

"I was looking for Sebastian, actually. Have you seen him? Oh, and a bottle of water, please." I smiled sweetly, resisting the urge to bat my eyelashes at him dramatically. They were amateur hour compared to Sebastian's anyway.

Keane set the bottle down on the counter between us with more force than was strictly necessary, sending a spattering of ice-cold condensation drops across my arm and clavicle. "$1.50. And no, I haven't."

I dug the money out of my pocket, which he slid off the counter brusquely, his eyes flicking over my head before snapping a none-too-subtle "Next!"

I bit back a smirk as I retreated to a table, mulling over the mental snapshots I'd need to bring that swirl of emotion to life. My gambit had worked better than I'd thought - there was definitely something either active or unrequited going on between Sebastian and Keane with a reaction like that. Attending an art school, I was certainly no stranger to boy drama, but I wasn't usually smack in the middle of it like this. As much fun as it was to poke the proverbial bear, I hoped I hadn't made trouble for Sebastian - or even Keane, for that matter. He may have been a dick, but no one needed to feel off-balance about someone they cared about.

Shoving down a twinge of guilt, I flipped to the page I'd been working on, eager to get down a distinctive line I'd noticed between Keane's brows. I noticed his glare twice more as I did my best to sit comfortably on the weathered picnic table bench, hunched over the table as I drew. When I was satisfied with the structure, I moved onto shading, sitting upright with a grumble of discomfort to stretch my lower back.

The quiet, hollow rustling sound didn't really register to my deep-in-art-process brain before a familiar, amused voice murmured at my ear, startling me.

"Well I'll be damned, Red. You've really captured the essence of bad-day Keane there."

I felt my already sun-warmed cheeks get even hotter as I twisted in my chair to face him, trying to cover my sketchbook with an arm reflexively. Did *Sebastian* think this was creepy? That'd be a real let-down because I'd maybe developed a little crush on the guy. Don't judge me, I was weak for curls.

"Oh! I, um, it's just that he's the right kind of model for one of my school assignments, that's all. Sorry. Would this bother him? I'll stop, I don't want to-"

Sebastian laughed, dropping into the chair across from me as he shook his head. "You're fine. It's probably better to keep it between us though, he hasn't had much of a sense of humor lately." A frown tilted his lips as he glanced over at the trailer, vanishing as his attention turned back to me. "But lucky me, I get to see you two days in a row, hm?"

I smiled at him, momentarily confused when I noted his usual bunch of balloons was nowhere to be found. That was strange, I could have sworn I'd heard them when he walked up behind me. "Well, we're getting to crunch time this semester, so I'm trying to get the work done I need to, and there's lots of inspiration here."

"I see." He rested his arms comfortably on the table between us. "So my sour-faced friend over there caught your eye, did he?" Sebastian's eyes glittered with mischievousness - I supposed it was karmic payback for my deliberately trying to get a rise out of Keane.

"Sure. There's other inspiration too, of course." I mirrored Sebastian's pose, resting my arms on the table and leaning down as a grin stretched across his lips. "You know, like the tamarins."

He laughed, clapping a hand to his heart like I'd shot him. "Ouch! Alright, alright, a man knows when he's been soundly beaten by adorable animals." His grin was infectious; if Keane was all dour shadows, Sebastian was closer to distilled sunshine. I normally didn't warm up to random guys so quickly, especially after the allergic-to-polite-refusals assholes on campus, but Sebastian was different. I liked his energy, it was...lighter, somehow.

A quick glance at my sketchbook told me I'd made enough progress; I could tidy Keane's image up at home and have it turn-in ready for tomorrow's class. That freed up some time to flirt with Sebastian a little. It was liberating being playful with a guy that felt safe, honestly - I wouldn't trust any of the idiots back at school not to follow me like an annoyingly persistent horny puppy.

"I guess you're okay too." I wrinkled my nose and tilted my hand back and forth in a so-so gesture.

He laughed so hard he coughed, and the sight of Sebastian practically gleeful made him even more attractive. I clearly did not get the full measure of his hotness yesterday, I'd been too busy melting and feeling anxious about Keane's chilly reception, which was unfortunately only metaphorical. I twisted off the cap to my water bottle without really thinking about it, passing it to Sebastian as he wheezed a little and took a sip.

He passed the bottle back over, the very tip of his tongue flicking deftly over his lower lip to catch a drop of water. I tried not to stare, but I *definitely* did. He cleared his throat and rolled his eyes dramatically. "The weather isn't the only thing that's brutal today. My poor ego. It's down for the count."

"Oh hush." It was shockingly easy to fall into warm familiarity with this man. I felt like I'd known him for months, and I didn't even know his last name yet. "You know damn well you're pretty, Sebastian. I don't know if that routine works on other girls, but the bashful act won't fly with me." I teasingly flicked the edge of his hand and raised a brow at him.

"Ohh, so the artist thinks I'm *pretty*, does she? Well, I'll have you know I can appreciate a work of art too." His eyes were nowhere near my sketchbook, and something in my lower stomach flipped pleasantly at his drop in tone. His voice softened further, a conspiratorial whisper. "And red just so happens to be my favorite color, by the way."

"Oh?" I took a long sip of the water, hoping it would cool the flush rising in my cheeks. "And how does Keane feel about your...art appreciation?" I offered the question cautiously, curious about the answer. Sebastian was a beautiful man, but I'd been cheated on before by an ex. I'd never inflict that pain on anyone, even if they were consistently a dick to me - it really wasn't cool, and I wouldn't enable it.

Several emotions flickered over Sebastian's face, and for a moment his usually wide-open expression was unreadable, confused. His brow furrowed, like it hadn't even occurred to him before I asked. "I - don't know, honestly. He wasn't happy yesterday."

"So -" I flipped to a blank page, doodling with my pencil for something to do. These felt like personal questions and I wondered if I was overstepping. *Keep it casual, Poppy.* "-are you two...together, or?"

Again that blank look, and a few blinks. "I mean, yes. We - well, we do what I've seen on-"

My nose burned as I choked on the mouthful of water I'd been taking. Sebastian had just name-dropped one of the raunchiest porn clip sites on the web like we were talking about the weather. He looked immediately concerned, coming over to gently thump on my back with an open palm, visibly relaxing when he saw me pull in a breath.

I whispered, voice raw from the coughing. "*Sebastian*, you can't just spring that on a girl!" I laughed, rubbing at an undoubtedly flaming-red cheek. Now my artist's brain was in overdrive, imagining the two of them at play. It was an extremely appealing mental sketch.

He grinned bashfully. "Sorry, what I meant was that we've been physically together for what feels like forever. I don't think we've ever called it anything in particular, though, if that's what you mean. We're not married, I don't think."

I snorted. Sebastian had a really weird sense of humor, but it was kind of endearing. "Well, you probably ought to figure out what you are, hon. Keane might think you are *something in particular*, that may be why he's not too fond of me, you know?"

I waited for that sly look, the one that guys that teased and poked at boundaries always seemed to wear, but Sebastian simply looked puzzled. Nearly introspective, really. He nodded absently, getting to his feet.

"You know, that's really good advice. I appreciate it, Red." He turned, getting ready to walk towards the concessions trailer. "Oh! Hey, before I forget - do you do drawings for money?"

I raised a brow at the sudden change in subject, and at the fact he was apparently just leaving the conversation without a goodbye. "Uh, commissions? Yeah, I mean, I guess I could take one on. I'm done with most of my involved coursework now for the semester."

"Ah, right, *commissions*. I didn't know the word. Well, if we gave you...hm." He tilted his head and stared off into space before looking back at me. "Five hundred dollars, could you make something very personal for Keane and I? It would be for our eyes only, and it's *very* important no one else sees it and you don't talk about it, okay?"

The smutty cogs in my brain started turning so fast they produced smoke. I answered before I'd really even thought about the question. Getting to sketch the two of them out NSFW-style for a month's rent? Sign me the fuck up. "Absolutely."

He smiled brightly, bobbing his head in a quick nod, his black curls bouncing with the movement. "Perfect. Will you be here tomorrow? Keane will let you know what he wants, and we might need to demonstrate a few things to make sure you get the line work right."

I felt light-headed. I held onto my water bottle like it was a lifeline, only barely resisting crushing it a little. "No - no I mean, I can come by Friday but I'll be, I mean, I have class. Stuff. I have class to do. For a test. In class." How could my tongue be simultaneously stuck to both the bottom *and* the roof of my mouth? On my wrist, my fitness watch gently vibrated to let me know my blood pressure was currently "in the zone" for aerobic activity. *No fuckin kidding.*

He nodded again, nibbling on his full lower lip as he looked thoughtfully over at the trailer. "That's okay, we can wait a little longer I think. I'm going to go tell Keane the good news - I'll see you here Friday and hey, good luck on your test!" He grinned and gave me a double thumbs-up before he walked away.

I glanced down to my sketchbook, where a pissed-off Keane stared back up at me from the table.

What the hell *was that?*

KEANE

It was only through sheer force of will that I didn't absolutely explode in anger at Seb as he clambered up the back steps. Not only was the goddamned redhead back, they'd been talking and laughing at the picnic table like I wasn't *right here*.

"Keane! I've got great news! Poppy is going to do our sigils for us!" He smiled brightly, expression dimming as he realized I was not at all happy with the development. "What's wrong, did something happen?"

I looked at him incredulously. "Seb, did I not tell you last night that I had it handled? I don't want *Poppy's* help. The way she looks at you is no better than Zina used to, like you're a goddamn corn dog to be devoured."

He folded his arms over his chest, scowling. It was completely unfamiliar body language from Seb, who I don't think I'd ever seen angry before. Scared, yes. Sad, definitely, but never angry. Until now, he'd been content to follow my lead - it was yet another thing that girl was interrupting. If she could cause this much chaos in only two days, that was more than enough proof that she was trouble.

Seb's tone was a new one too. It was serious, and entirely unlike the man I knew. "That's my concern though, isn't it? You know that Poppy asked me what we were, and I didn't even know what to tell her? What are we, Keane? I've been following you for so long and I've never questioned where you were leading us, but you - it's like you want to *keep* me like *she* did." His voice thickened, big brown eyes watering with emotion that tangled in his lashes.

I could almost hear my own heart crack in the sterile, air-conditioned chill of the trailer. "Seb - Sebastian, love. Oh no, I'm so sorry." I closed the distance between us in a step, pulling him into my arms and crushing him against my chest. "You are everything to me, and don't you ever, ever doubt that. You're my whole world, Seb. I just want you happy, I don't want anyone to hurt you, and if Zina can...hold us that way, Poppy might be able to as well, can't you understand that? I'm trying to *protect* us."

He sniffled against my shoulder, cuddling closer in my arms. "She's different, Keane, she's not going to hurt us. She'll help us escape for good, she even promised she'd never tell anyone what we asked her to draw. I told her you'd want to demonstrate what we need, too, so we can hopefully get it right the first time."

It took a lot of willpower not to tense with irritation. Seb was right, I had been calling the shots this whole time, but hadn't he let me? Hadn't I kept us safe? There wasn't a way of untangling our plan from this girl, now - he'd gone against my wishes and, short of a direct demand that probably wouldn't go over well, I didn't see a way out.

Unless *I* found what we needed before the girl could shove her way into our lives again. If someone *else* drew the sigils, there was no reason at all for her to hover around Sebastian. I'd have to work fast, though - now that I was racing both our protective spell and that redheaded interloper, urgency was expanding my chest in all the wrong ways.

I kissed Sebastian's temple and slid away from him, glancing at the trailer door. Fortunately, we were both slated to work in the trailer today, and he could cover for me. "Seb, I need to go see if the library has a book I've been tracking down. Can you manage here alone for a few hours?"

Seb looked confused at the sudden change in topic, but nodded. "Of course. Should be slow today, it's supposed to rain. Just be careful?"

I smiled reassuringly, confident I'd be able to fix our problems before sunset. I'd already tracked down the last bit of lore we'd need - with a little luck and a steady, living hand helping us, Seb and I could be *truly* free. Sure, he'd probably be irritated at me for cutting Poppy out, but what was some little infatuation compared to actual freedom? No more fear, no more hiding, no more breathlessly waiting to be caught.

With another quick hug - Seb and I had discovered early on that some people didn't approve of two men embracing - I slipped out of the trailer. I wasn't wearing our garish uniform today, and I'd shrugged off the brightly-colored vest before I left. When we'd fled, it had been with only the baggy linen-like trousers and tunics we wore with the circus - not exactly a discreet look when trying to stay hidden. Our first discreet envelope of "under the table" pay from the zoo had gone to some jeans and t-shirts, much better clothing in terms of discretion. The striped zoo uniforms we had to wear outside the trailer felt constricting, so I only wore mine when I absolutely had to.

I blended into a large group heading towards the bus

parking lot and caught a public bus heading into the nearby city. I assumed the girl - Poppy - attended the nearby Arts College of Twin Arbor River. From what I'd overheard and seen during zoo tours, it was the most logical place to start my search for an artist. The trick would be finding the right *kind* of artist - a sculptor wouldn't do us a bit of good.

I frowned out the bus window, closing my eyes and allowing my senses to roam the boundaries of our current sigil-spell. It was a little stronger than I'd feared, but the degradation was unmistakable: we had maybe a week before it would crumble altogether. I wouldn't go back to Zina, wouldn't let her pull Seb back into her clutches. I'd sooner deflate myself. She'd been getting meaner, towards the end. When she had too much to drink - more nights than not - she took special glee in threatening Seb's life. As much as I tried to keep my expressions neutral during her drunken rampages, she knew I cared about him. Zina knew *he* was the way to hurt me when her scratches, pinches, and slaps failed to get the reaction she craved out of me. She just hadn't realized that my feelings were more than fraternal protectiveness - I shuddered to think what might have happened if she'd found out earlier.

A loud chime pulled me out of my reverie, the bus jerking to a stop across the street from the college. I filed out along with a knot of chattering students, following ponytails and buzzcuts in every color of the rainbow. I did like that about the artistic humans, their love of bright hues. My own brilliant royal purple hue was a point of pride whenever I shifted.

I followed the meandering pack in the side doors of the school, grateful I could slip in after I spotted one using a key card. Once they scattered and wandered off down different hallways, however, I was lost. My plan wasn't well-formed from here; I only knew I needed an artist, but how did one start looking in a place like this?

A loud finger snap caught my attention, echoing down the hall. A peeved-looking older man with wildly unkempt black hair glared at me from a nearby doorway. "Come on - you're already ten minutes late, let's *go*." He stabbed a finger towards the room he'd come from, brow raised.

Caught someplace I shouldn't be without any real explanation, I followed his direction, trying my best to look like I belonged there. A soft purple robe was shoved into my hands as the man flung a hand over his head in exasperation. "Get undressed, robe on, out the side door, you know the drill. Move it, because they're already getting restless."

He stomped out, the heavy door he'd indicated thumping in his wake.

I blinked, staring at the robe in my hands. It wasn't that I was concerned about my nudity - Zina had made both Seb and I exceptional by human standards, for obvious reasons - but rather confused as to why it was called for here. I moved to try the door to the hallway, but found the only handle to be a dimly-lit indicator sign that it was a fire door. I wasn't sure how the man had opened it without an alarm moments ago, but I didn't want to risk triggering it by mistake. Looked like I was getting naked.

I methodically stripped down, folding my clothes in a pile and wondering who "they" were on the other side of the smaller door. Obviously artists of some sort, but I wasn't sure why I'd need to get naked for that. I pulled on the robe, smiling despite the day's tension. It was gloriously soft, unlike anything I'd ever worn before, and it felt amazing. I allowed a small circle of flesh on my arm to shift, the short, silky fibers of the robe brushing my royal purple balloon-skin with a comforting susurration. The sensation helped settle my nerves, and, after tying the robe securely around my waist, I gently pushed the side door open, blinking my way into a much larger, brighter classroom.

The older man that had ushered me into the first room

peeked around the edge of a canvas, giving a small nod of approval. When I didn't move, he tilted his head towards a dias-like raised bed in the center of the room, raising a brow. What on earth was this? Was he forcing me to perform as Zina did? No one else was on the bed-like counter, just a thin padded mat and a pillow.

Was I expected to perform...alone? Zina had made me do that once before deciding she didn't care for it, even if I secretly preferred it to her touch. Judging by the mix of easels and sketchbooks around the dias, it was clear the class would be using me as a model, though I'd never heard of a *naked* model before.

The older man cleared his throat sharply. "Welcome to Advanced Figure Drawing, Mr. Bilbrey. Please disrobe and take your place, the class is eager to use their workshop time. I'll have Andrea bring you some water."

I nodded nervously, tugging loose the belt of the robe and climbing up onto the raised bed before letting it fall completely away from my body. I dropped the soft purple off the far side of the dias, away from the semicircle of students around me. Unsure what the older man wanted me to do, I leaned back, crossing my arms behind my head on the pillow, just as I'd relax if I was back in Zina's trailer. Seb and I hadn't slept in a real bed since escaping, and sometimes I missed the soft comfort of it.

There were a few barely-audible murmurs as I stretched out, causing the man to clear his throat again. "Class, let's have some professionalism, please. Be grateful for the range of models you've had this semester so far, and let's get to work."

A young woman, cheeks burning, brought me a cold bottle of water without looking at me directly. I gave her a small nod of thanks and took a sip before getting back in position, setting the bottle down beside the robe. The door to the classroom opened with a harsh squeak, and a familiar head of red hair ducked in, already rambling some sort of explanation or excuse. *Just my goddamn luck.*

"Professor Anders, I'm so sorry, I just got off the phone with Margot and there's some kind of passport issue, so-" Poppy cut off abruptly, registering that there was a body on the dias where she clearly hadn't been expecting one, and also that the body was *me*.

The older man - Professor Anders, evidently - gave her a confused look. "What do you mean, Poppy? Mr. Bilbrey's here, admittedly he cut it a little close, but...?" He squinted at me, tilting his head. "And now that I think about it, have you already been working with him? Mr. Bilbrey is your week's model, isn't he? If not, they could practically be twins."

To her credit, Poppy recovered quickly. "Oh, uhm, yes. I - well, honestly, I forgot we'd already worked out a replacement for William while he was on vacation. Silly of me, I apologize. And yes, you're absolutely right...Keane sat for me this week. He's got very interesting lines, don't you think?"

"Mm." Professor Anders didn't seem impressed, but nodded towards an empty seat, which Poppy quickly scurried to, pulling out her sketchbook. With so many students watching and sketching, I couldn't shoot her the angry look I wanted to, but I did lock eyes with her for a long, uncomfortable moment. Good, she could squirm for all I cared. She'd been a thorn in my side since the moment Seb had dragged her into my trailer.

I tried to remain still after a few quiet corrections from the Professor, and a panicked look or two from Poppy over the next hour or so. I could have admitted I wasn't who they thought I was and left, but it likely would have prevented me from getting the help I came here for. Additionally, my continual presence seemed to be turning Poppy into a nervous wreck, so that was a nice side-effect.

It wasn't to say I wasn't relieved when the Professor finally called time, motioning for me to slide the robe on again as the students filtered out. "Mr. Bilbrey, I would appreciate it if you could be more conscious about time for your next session, but I appreciate your commitment. You were excellent at holding your pose. Poppy? Would you mind letting Mr. Bilbrey back into the storeroom? I need to get to an appointment."

She flicked her sketchbook closed, nodding as she held it to her chest, staying in place until the Professor had left. I fell into step beside her as she crossed the room, her knuckle-white grip on her sketchbook showing her nerves. "Keane, what the actual hell are you doing here? I know damn well you're not Drew Bilbrey, and thank God Prof Anders didn't."

I smirked, rolling my shoulders in a shrug. "You come and bother me at my job, I figured I'd return the favor."

She scowled, looking over her shoulders nervously before unlocking and shoving the storeroom door open, gesturing with her sketchbook for me to pass. I slipped past her, not bothering to create space between us in the doorway. I was, strangely enough, becoming a fan of flustered Poppy. Off-balance like this, she felt like less of a problem and more of a…diversion. Something interesting beyond inventories of soda bottles and the endless stress of the protective sigils.

When I unceremoniously dropped the robe into a puddle on the floor, her audible gasp and rapid flick of her eyes down my body, then frantically away, piqued my interest. I'd assumed she was chasing Seb, and perhaps she was, but hadn't the Professor said about her drawing me previously?

"Is there a problem, Poppy? You just spent the last two hours staring at me naked, seems a little disingenuous to blush now." I grinned wickedly, crossing my arms over my chest and making no move to get my clothes.

"Yes, when you were a *model, Keane*. Did you really come

here to...to stalk me or something? If this is about Seb..." She swallowed and snapped her eyes to mine, her chin taking on a defiant tilt. Spitfire of a girl, this one - it wasn't unappealing, I supposed. I could, reluctantly, admit that Seb wasn't wrong to find her intriguing.

But still - I'd come here for a reason, and it was to get her the hell out of our lives. "It is about Seb, as a matter of fact. He's mine, and I'd appreciate it if you would stop flirting with him."

Her jaw tensed, hurt flashing momentarily through her eyes. "Well, fine, but I didn't approach him, you know. He was the one that's been hitting on me. Hell *I* was the one that pumped the brakes by asking what was going on with the two of you - I'm not interested in coming between anyone, Keane. I'm sorry if I did."

The way her shoulders dropped made this little game less fun. Something suspiciously like guilt crept into my stomach and I reached for my clothes. "It's...that's alright. I'm sorry if I made you uncomfortable."

She laughed softly, shaking her head. "I wouldn't call it uncomfortable, exactly. I'm glad to clear the air, though - I didn't want there to be bad blood while I'm trying to sketch you two on Friday."

I frowned, zipping up and buttoning my pants before turning back to her. "Why would you sketch us? Seb told you what we need, didn't he?"

She blinked, eyes dropping to her sketchbook as she bit her lip. "Well, I mean, I thought he did? He said it was something very personal to the two of you, and he swore me to secrecy, so I just assumed..."

I know I'd just gotten done apologizing for teasing her, but when she made it so easy, I couldn't be blamed for taking the bait. "Assumed what, Poppy?"

"You wanted a...you know...an *adult* drawing of the two of you...together?" Her voice crept up an octave and she winced at me.

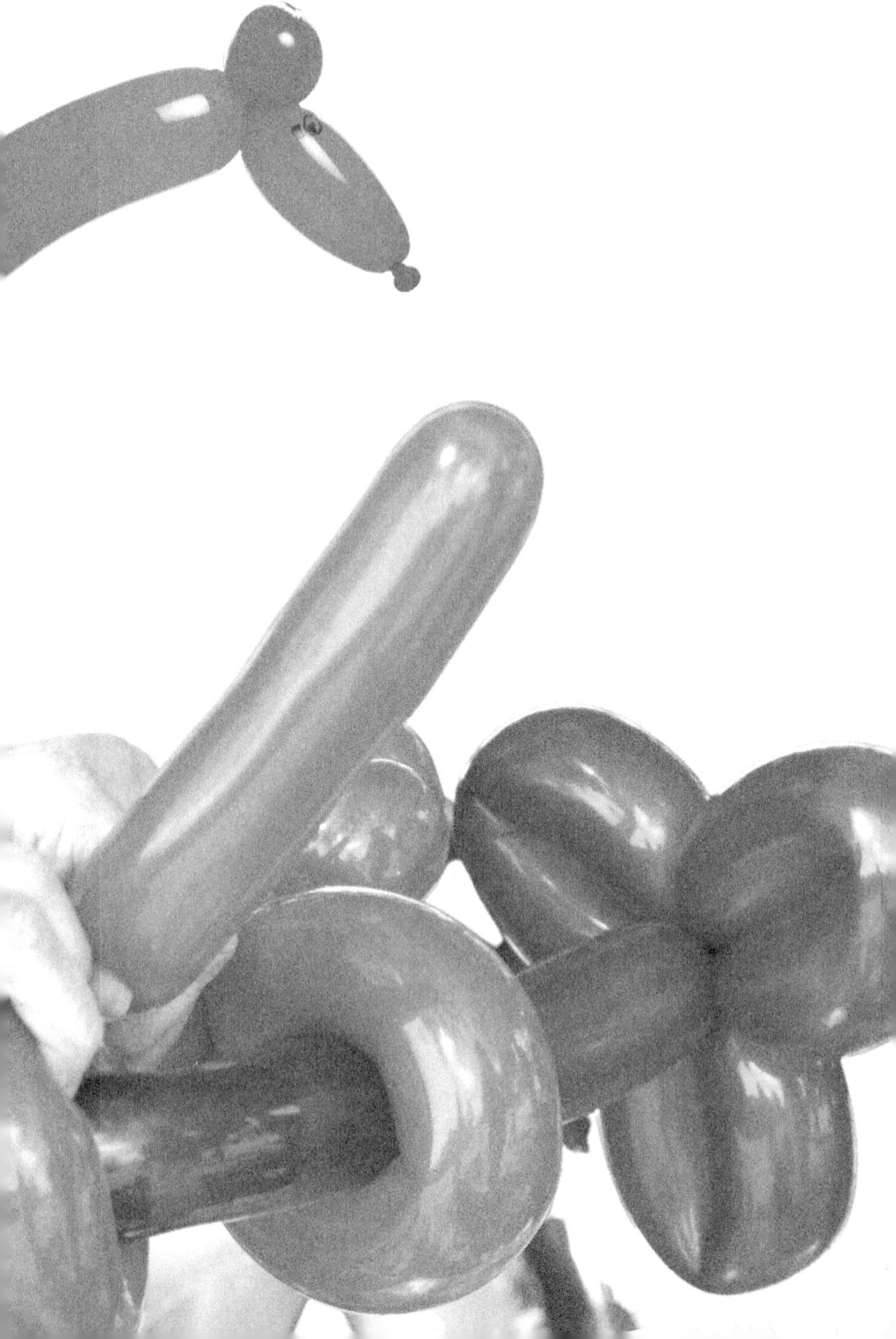

POPPY

Oh god. Oh *god*.

Had I really misunderstood Sebastian that badly, and just *admitted* it to Keane? He still stood there, shirtless and stupidly hot, a bemused expression softening his features as things clicked into place for him.

"Ahh. And when Seb told you I wanted to demonstrate what we wanted, you thought-" Something wicked danced in his eyes as he moved a step closer.

Was it hot in here? It felt hot in here. My stupid goddamn fitness watch buzzed again and I tore it off and chucked it into a box of rulers. Fucking snitch.

"Look, Keane, I don't know! He's hot, you're hot, I'm good at drawing and it just seemed like...you know, like maybe I'd get money and a fun party story out of it. I don't *know*. It sounds dumb now that I'm saying it out loud." I hissed an aggrieved sigh and shoved a hand through my hair, embarrassment burning through me. I can't believe I'd jumped to a conclusion like that - I decided I was going to blame it on sun exposure if Keane pressed me.

"You think I'm hot, do you?" His smile was the kind of predatory that made it hard to stand still. I wasn't afraid, not really, but Keane seemed to enjoy keeping me guessing - what he'd say next, what he'd do next. "Is that why you've been sketching me?"

Ah fuck. He heard the Prof.

My heart thudded in my chest as he stepped closer, in my space now. "I needed a stern model and you frowned at me a lot. So sue me. If it bothers you I won't -"

The tiny storeroom was hot, but Keane's mouth was hotter as it unexpectedly claimed mine, all self-assured confidence that invited me to melt into it, words lost in the unfairly talented twist of his tongue. He broke off the kiss after a blissfully long moment, resting his forehead on mine, his voice a low growl. "You are annoying, persistent, and beautiful. I see what Seb sees in you."

That heat slid straight between my legs at his words, a strange mix of insult and praise. "Thanks?"

He chuckled, twining his fingers in the back of my hair with a casual possessiveness that, I was ashamed to admit, damn near had me panting. "We do not need *adult* drawings, Poppy. I need you to draw special sigils, and the linework is precise. Can you do that for me? For Seb and I?"

I nodded mutely, trying to concentrate on his words instead of the hot press of his body, trapping me against the metal storage rack behind us. "And Seb told you we had money for you, yes?" A long, dextrous finger twined a lock of my hair at the nape of my neck. I managed another nod.

Keane's lips practically burned down the side of my neck, which I very happily exposed to him. This is *not* how I thought the day was going to go, but damned if I wasn't happy to let this particular scenario play out. "A woman tried to come between Seb and I before, Poppy, and it's never going to happen again. I'm going to get the upper hand this time, you understand me?"

He gave a soft tug to my hair and I swallowed a groan. "Yes. Yes, please." I didn't even know what the hell I was asking for, but I'd never been so wet in my damn *life*. My brain might still consider Keane an unredeemable douchecanoe, but my body was ready to run through a field of flags as red as my namesake to get to him.

His hand hit the wall to the side of the rack as our lips crashed together again, the errant light switch plunging the tiny room into darkness. That was just fine with me, Keane felt like a dirty, illicit secret I couldn't wait to explore. Fuck, I could lose my goddamn placement if they found out I was fucking around with a model - but *Keane wasn't a model*, right? I clung to that paper-thin justification as closely as the man himself, currently grinding his hips into me at just the right angle.

"Fuck, why do you smell so good?" There was that growl again, evaporating every last ounce of sense in my head. Hell, I could ask him the same thing - there was the faintest whiff of burnt sugar, something like dessert wafting off of him. Previous models had smelled of soap, and more often BO after a long session under the lights, but not Keane. No, he was as infuriatingly delicious in scent as he was visually and I wanted to lick him more than anything on earth right now.

I tapped the metal rack with an open palm, using it to navigate and clumsily dragging Keane with me as we kissed hungrily. I pulled the two of us down onto a pile of blankets and folded mats we used on the dias in the classroom - it was lumpy but it'd do for now.

Keane shoved his pants off with the same speed he'd put them on, hesitating at my own fly as I pushed my shoes off. I pressed his hand into the button at my waist, whimpering with a sudden, overwhelming need. My clothes were too tight, too constricting - I needed to be naked, I needed Keane, and I needed him in me. He slid them off, and I kicked them free impatiently, reaching for him.

"Shhh...easy. I'm going to take care of you." His voice had become softer, deeper, and even in the dark I could feel the intensity of his gaze on my skin. Defying anything resembling logic, I believed him. I knew he'd take care of me, I knew he'd help with this sudden intense urge that made me want to crawl out of my own skin. *What the hell was going on?*

My fingers slid down the flat plane of his stomach, brushing his inner thigh as his mouth devoured mine. "Poppy - breathe. Share your breath with me. Please." Keane's tone was sweetly pleading, the voice of a man on the edge of utterly losing it. Maybe it was some kind of kink, I thought through the haze of lust. I did as he asked, breathing into him with our next kiss, his wild moan vibrating on my lips.

His cock lay like a branding iron on my inner thigh, strangely smooth. Had he put on a condom? I relaxed into the mats, grateful we wouldn't have to stop to do so - he was *fast* with it, I hadn't even felt him get protection out. It *was* dark in here, though.

"Poppy, are - can I?" His fingers slid without preamble between my legs, where I was so slick now I'd have been embarrassed if I wasn't lust-drunk. As it was, I pressed my hand on top of his happily, pushing myself against that glorious contact with a small, tight sound of assent. He growled again, and his touch abruptly vanished as a wet click sounded, followed by the unmistakable sounds of lapping. My hips arched of their own accord as I realized he was tasting me on his fingers. He grabbed my waist and dragged me down the mats, guiding one of my thighs over his shoulder as he stretched out on his stomach. It was all the warning I had before his mouth met my cunt, making me even more of a mess with his lips, tongue and teeth.

I reached down and roughly fisted his hair, whimpering again as I tried to ride his face, desperate for contact, for release, for *something*. Two fingers delved deep into me, curling and stroking as he purred against my skin, kissing soft my inner thigh. "Come for me, sweet little flower, let me taste you. It'll make it easier to take me."

A faint curl of confusion at his words seeped into my mind before an orgasm obliterated anything but the rhythmic stroke of Keane's tongue, the insistent press of his fingers, and the way his body bore down on me. "Good....so good. So beautiful for me." He cooed the words soft and sweet, making my brain go pleasantly hazy.

He moved fluidly onto his knees between my legs, gently lifting my thighs to wrap around his hips. His hand tightened on my arm, face nuzzling beside mine, drawing deep breaths like he was addicted to the smell of me. "Poppy - I want...please..."

I slid a hand between us, opening myself for him, pleased at the shuddering breath he pulled beside my ear as he nudged forward at my invitation. Every one of the muscles under my seeking, stroking fingertips was corded tight, like holding back required every last thread of his self-control. I enjoyed that power, the way it made me feel, and I wanted to see him undone. I *would* see him undone. Pulling my heels against his back, I drew him into me, more and more, every last inch of that impressive shaft that had set half my class to wide-eyed blushing.

Just when I thought he was buried in me, there was more - twice, I was convinced he had bottomed out, and twice I was wrong. Then, something wide and soft bumped against my clit, making my toes curl with a surge of pleasure. What the hell was *that*? I opened my mouth to ask, to pause, to figure out what it was that felt so good, but something deeper in my soul wrenched control from my conscious mind. It was *necessary*, whatever it was, and I would have it. It was mine to take.

Keane was mine to take.

The moment that inviting bulge forced its way in - half through the tightening of my legs, half through the pleasantly single-minded drive of Keane's hips - my teeth found his shoulder. I'd never been a biter or scratcher during sex but Keane had unlocked something primal in me. I tasted the skin I'd wanted to, and sank my teeth into his flesh happily, feeling unbelievably, cosmically *right* about it. It was a shallow bite, but the faint taste of copper told me I apparently hadn't fucked around about it. He tasted as sweet as caramel, which was completely impossible, and my senses filled with a soft hiss and a whiff of ozone.

With one more powerful drive of his hips, that bulge locked up tight against my G-spot, sending me gushing arousal in the most powerful, puzzling climax of my life. A sharp squeaking sound filled the room as he rocked against me, eagerly chasing his peak. A sharp pinch on my shoulder and Keane's hot breath accompanied the undeniable tension and groan of his own climax, complete with a warm gush deep inside me.

I dropped my head back heavily on a dusty cushion, panting like I'd just run a goddamn marathon. "Jesus....fucking hell, Keane. Where the hell did *that* come from? I thought you hated me."

He didn't respond, but drew me into an embrace and rolled us, letting me rest on top of his body as he stroked my back. His cock was still in me, which was strange - I'd had several lovers in my time, and they'd all physically withdrawn by this point, even if we were cuddling after. I decided I liked it, the fullness of it. But what the fuck *was* it?

I awkwardly patted up the wall, my fingertips just barely brushing the switch, flooding the small storeroom with light. We were a goddamn *mess*, and both Keane and I had a shoulder smeared with blood. *Oh shit, we actually* bit *each other*.

Panic started tapping at my brain - we'd had safe sex but here we were exchanging goddamn blood borne pathogens, how could I be so stupid? How could *he* be so stupid? "Keane - Keane, fuck, we're bleeding, oh my god. I - do you have, I mean - I don't have any STIs or anything but this isn't good. Do you have any medical issues?" I clapped a hand to where he'd bitten me, feeling the small wound.

He sighed deeply, looking up at me like we'd known each other for a lifetime, gently reaching for my hands and interlacing our fingers. "Poppy, you're safe, but we really need to talk."

He tilted his hips and nodded downwards, where his entire pelvic region - still locked into my own - had gone a deep royal purple.

And translucent.

I screamed.

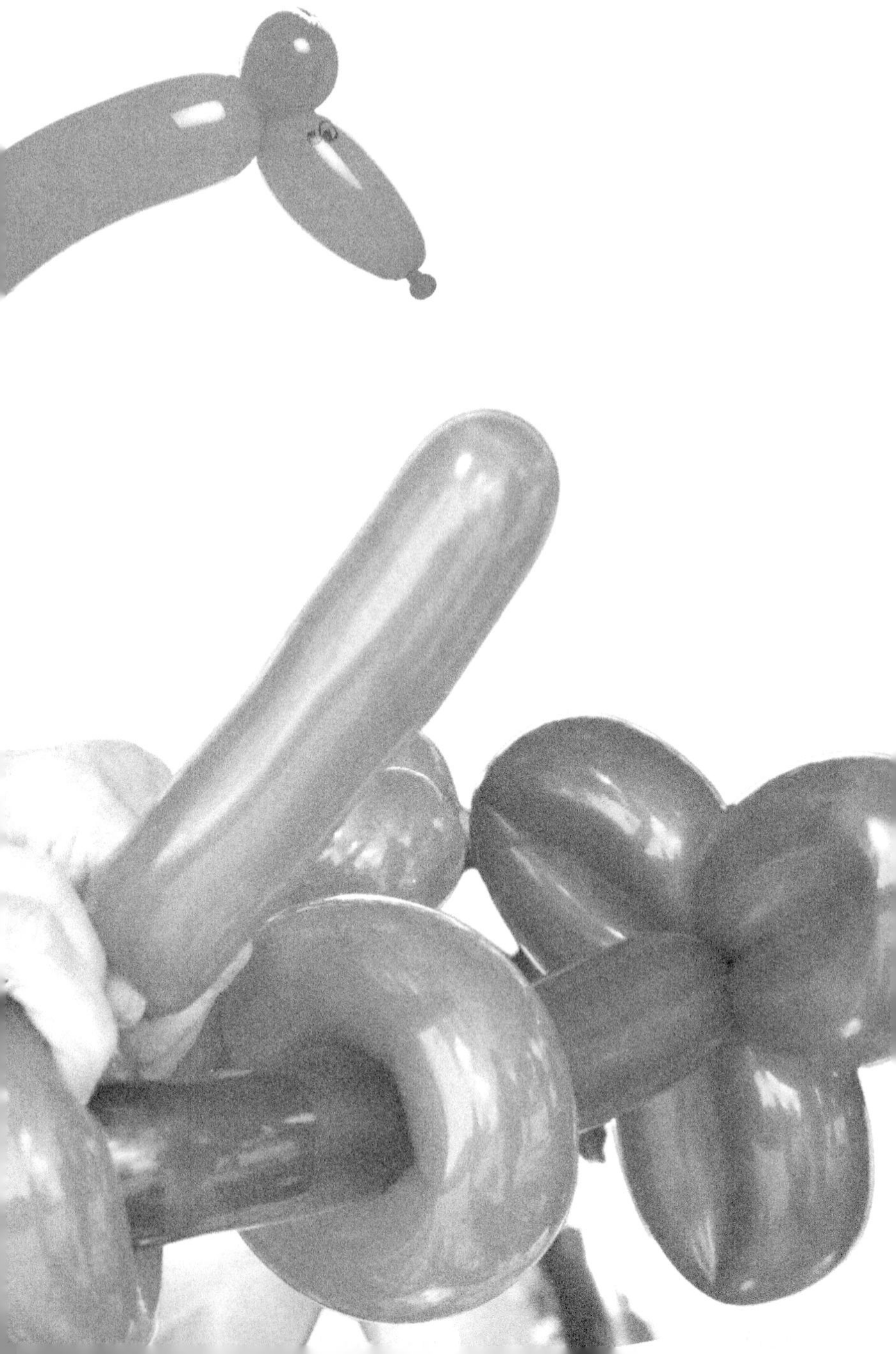

SEBASTIAN

Keane had reappeared at the trailer several hours after he left, hair and clothes wildly disheveled, a faint trace of blood on his neck and shoulder where he'd tried to clean it up.

Grateful it was closing time anyway, I flicked the window and blinds closed, worried sick about him - did Zina already find us? Had he been attacked?

The last thing on earth I expected to see was a similarly-disheveled Poppy hauled into the trailer behind him before he shut the door frantically. She looked shell-shocked, and was clinging to Keane's hand like they didn't absolutely loathe each other this morning.

"What the fuck happened, Keane? Are you okay? Is - is Poppy okay?" I widened my eyes at him and he shook his head dismissively.

"She knows, Seb. I mean, I gave her the crash course on the

way over, but she knows. It's...well, it's as fine as it can be. She's still going to help us, but something weird happened." He looked as startled as she did, and more than a little guilty.

I sighed heavily. "Keane, in all your research, did you ever think to read the red book? Once you found out why you and I could...be with one another?" The small red book dealt with sex magic and the dominion Zina had over us. The spells within it weren't the magic that brought us into being, but they were undeniably the ones she used to bring us to heel.

I looked at Poppy - she was probably scared out of her mind. Bites like that told me Keane had knotted her, which could only mean one thing. She was an *actual* tulpamancer, an omega to our alpha natures. And, more importantly, she was now mated, however unintentionally, to Keane.

Keane shook his head, looking to *me* for answers for a change. It was a role reversal I didn't have time to savor right now, as their impulsive mating had just added a significant new wrinkle to our permanent escape plan. "Poppy must be a latent tulpamancer, Keane. Not borrowed magic, not like Zina, a *real* one. Those are mating bites you've given each other, and that means she's managed to do by accident what Zina had been trying to do on purpose for years. You two are permanently bonded."

"I...what? That's crazy. There's no way. I don't know what magic tricks you two are doing with the...purple skin...thing and the strange penis whatever he has going on, but I don't *do* drugs and I have a college career and..." Poppy looked dangerously close to hyperventilating, her eyes darting all over the trailer.

I smiled sadly. I couldn't help feeling jealous that someone else now had what I'd always craved from Keane. Unfortunately, one of the drawbacks of being a creation was that we couldn't bond with other creations, just living tulpamancers. I held up a hand to pause her spiraling thoughts. "Keane, purr for her. Your omega is distressed, alpha. Do what you know you need to."

Keane's eyes were panicked too, but instinct swept in to smooth the rough edges of this very real shitshow of a situation. As soon as he started the deep, quiet rumble of a sound, I watched tension drain out of Poppy until she cuddled up to him with a contented sigh. She smiled and blinked sleepily, and I smirked despite myself - they were so pretty together. It left me the odd man out, but that was alright - Keane was safe, and that's what mattered most to me.

I shuffled closer to them, coaxing us all to sit on the floor of the trailer. I held Keane's free hand, because I wasn't sure how much longer I'd get to, and I needed comfort too. "You're free, Keane. You know that, don't you? You can't belong to more than one tulpamancer, and unless Poppy releases you to another with a ritual, Zina can't compel you anymore."

Keane couldn't look more shocked if he tried. "What, you're saying that just because Poppy and I...?"

I shrugged and smiled, squeezing his hand. "According to the red book, Tulpamancers - natural ones - are insanely rare. It might have even been her latent magic pulling me in her direction in the first place, for all I know. Even entirely untrained, she trumps Zina any day of the week. There's no chance borrowed magic can nullify your new bond, Keane."

Poppy leaned her temple against Keane's arm - this early on in the bond, they'd be driven to stay in close contact. "What Keane told me, though - this...this Zina of yours, isn't she coming for you too? We have to keep you safe, Sebastian."

My heart, created though it was, skipped a beat. I assumed they'd want to settle down somewhere as a pair, I'd already been mentally preparing myself to be ousted. The book was clear in that the relationships between tulpamancers and their creations immediately took precedence over any and all others previously in their lives. It was one of the reasons the magic was relatively rare - it was a giving of *two* sides, rather than the one-sided control offered by most summoning magic. Zina had been working to pervert the idea of the tulpa bond to the latter sort, which is why I suspected she'd always failed.

Which brought up another interesting conundrum. Keane hadn't made me leave - in fact, he'd come *to* me. According to the red book, Poppy should be in heat right now, and Keane should be in rut - eyes only for one another for a few days until the bond solidified.

Keane still held Poppy tight to his side, half in his lap, and neither of them looked like they were going anywhere. I leaned in, cautiously, pressing my lips to Keane's. He dropped my hand and used his palm to caress my cheek like he always did, kissing me deeply until I was almost dizzy.

When I rocked back, there was nothing but pleasant heat in Poppy's eyes, and the same look of want Keane always seemed to have around me. This was impossible, according to the lore, but here it was happening right in front of me. What should have been a mated pair was making ample room for me, right when they would normally be homicidally vicious about defending their pairing and nest.

Ah, shit, a nest. I'd never even considered that part, because after our first and only experience with a theoretical tulpamancer, Keane and I had no interest in ever meeting another. Poppy was an unexpected addition to our lives, and our saving grace, all at once. While my own Alpha nature was less prominent than Keane's, it was still reacting to the presence of an omega - even a sated one.

"Keane, we need to get Poppy a nest, I don't think she's going to feel safe or comfortable out in the open for a few days. Poppy, sweetheart, do you have a home? Keane and I don't really have a need for one, so we can't give you the nest you'll need right now." I cautiously stroked the outside of her arm, unbelievably relieved when she seemed to welcome it.

Could this actually work?

She nodded, eyes darting back and forth between the two of us uncertainly. Keane and I both growled, protective instincts forcing us to search out whatever threatened her. Shit, *we* needed to get into her nest before we hurt someone as a perceived threat.

With a hastily-scribbled note about food poisoning, Poppy grabbed each of our hands and hustled us to her car, flushed and panting. The heat cycle the two of them had kicked off meant Poppy would be horribly uncomfortable without regular physical satisfaction. It was a mechanism meant to encourage newly-formed bond pairs to mate and knot, becoming attached in both a literal and metaphysical sense.

I was pleasantly surprised when Poppy reclined the driver's seat of her car, dragging me closer by the front of my shirt and kissing me deeply. She shimmied her pants down off her hips and tugged Keane's hand down into the parted denim, gasping with pleasure as his fingers slid deep into her.

"Just...help me take the edge off, both of you, please." I found a windshield screen in the back and unfolded the shiny silver accordion over us as best I could, thankful she'd parked in a remote corner of the lot to begin with. We needed to get her into a nest *soon*. I could already feel my own senses start to haze into rut - once she mated me, and hopefully she would, I'd be just as dazed as Keane.

Keane obediently worked her into a powerful frenzy, and I couldn't resist tugging up her shirt and bra to mouth and tongue her nipples. Keane joined me by treating her other breast, and together we brought her to a panting, whining climax that left his palm utterly drenched. I licked his fingers clean, sharing kisses with both Poppy and Keane until she felt calm enough to drive.

Back at Poppy's apartment, in a brief window of lucidity, we'd agreed to try an additional mate bond. What she'd done with Keane couldn't be undone, and he and I didn't want to leave one another. Hearing Keane declare his love for me, knowing he was in full rut with his omega mate, was the only proof I'd ever need that he well and truly loved me. Not because of shared trauma or even magical makeup, but because of who we were as created beings.

We dragged every soft pillow, blanket, and throw in her apartment into the bedroom, making a soft, dimly-lit divot for the three of us to ride out the heat cycle. I breathlessly watched Poppy and Keane enjoy another round with one another, a little sense coming back to her as his knot soothed her wild omega needs. In that clarity, she reached for me, her deliberate bite soft and tender, almost loving, against my shoulder. It was the same place she'd bitten Keane, and my heart thrilled to match them both.

Keane and I showed Poppy how to kiss and pull breath back to adjust our knots, if she wanted, but her smile told me she wouldn't be doing that often. She did it in the nest, however, to make room for me. I drew her legs up onto my shoulders as I slid in, a freshly-satiated Keane holding my base to offer us the perfect glide of connection. When I bent down to gently bite the soft, delectable flesh of her thigh against my shoulder, I knew precisely what I'd been created for: this.

Three days later, having carefully kept Poppy fed, bathed, and hydrated between bouts, the mindless drive started to ease its delightful hold on us. Rather than dim our passion, however, it simply allowed us to be more imaginative in our connections. Poppy, after an initial adjustment period, had marveled over how bright and colorful we were in partial shift, pulling us over to fuck by the windows so she could watch the slant of deep purple and bright red sunlight through our translucent, hollow bodies.

With a mischievous grin, she aggressively wrestled me on the carpet for long moments, giggling wildly. When I caught my breath from laughing, she shoved me against the wall, bending over in front of me and taunting me to take her again. As eager as I was, I couldn't move a muscle, a predicament that Keane laughed uproariously at - she called the magic *static electricity* and seemed oddly excited it 'finally messed up my perfect hair.' While I should have hated it, I secretly loved being forced to watch her with Keane while I couldn't even give myself relief. While the effects of her strange magic wore off, Keane pushed her down on all fours where I could see everything, taking her from behind with the beautiful, passionate sound of squeaking latex echoing through her apartment, accompanied by Poppy's ecstatic moans.

We'd eventually figured out that a tulpamancer could change our shape in very interesting ways, too. With deft fingers, and several assurances nothing hurt, she'd twisted Keane's shaft into a temporary row of small, round bubbles instead of the thick column that both she and I were so fond of. After that had come the pleasant revelation that she enjoyed something else I did, too. As I buried myself knot-deep in her cunt from underneath her, Keane teased and penetrated her ass one small sculpted bubble at a time, pulling out at her moment of climax exactly as she'd begged us to.

On the last day of Poppy's heat, Zina finally found us. By then, it was far too late - our bonds were well and truly sealed, and even our old keeper's dramatic door-crashing entrance into Poppy's apartment couldn't separate our new family.

Heat-deadly and furious, our omega tulpamancer let instinct guide her in removing a rival from her nest, shoving our former tormentor out into the balcony. Once there, she simply grabbed her by the hair, pressing a disgusted, loveless kiss to her lips - a kiss of death, from one true tulpamancer to a false one.

Both Keane and I learned something in that moment. Humans certainly weren't *meant* to be filled with helium, but *could* be with enough determination. And if you filled them with *enough* helium, they'd literally float away until they became the airless stratosphere's problem, rather than the earth's.

We closed the balcony doors, Poppy brushed her teeth half a dozen times, and we settled back into the nest. It was a strange and beautiful happily ever after, and we made it our solemn mission - even after the heat ended - to find out all the ways that two balloons and an open-minded, mostly-human woman could twist themselves up in pleasure.

Want to know what comes next for our semi-inflatable trio? By popular demand, the story of Poppy, Sebastian, and Keane will continue in *Squeal*, **debuting May 2023!**

About Vera Valentine

An unapologetic book-huffer and devourer-of-stories, Vera Valentine has carried on a torrid love affair with the written word for nearly all of her 40 years. Grown in the diner-laden wilds of the New Jersey Pine Barrens and transplanted to North Carolina, she lives with her husband, eight cats, and two dogs, most of whom are house trained. An avid fan of the Paranormal Why Choose genre, she tossed her author hat into the ring in September of 2021 and never looked back.

A self-professed chaotic capybara, Vera can usually be found spending too much time on social media, chilling with fellow authors, or scribbling down ever-expanding plot bunny ideas in her trusty paper sidekick, the Bad Idea Book™.

If you'd like to stay up-to-date on Vera's latest projects and preorders, stop by her website - ValentineVerse.com for information, links, newsletter signups, ARC opportunities, and more!

ALSO BY VERA VALENTINE

The Carnal Cryptids Series

Squeak

Sap and Spile

Hayseed

The Holiday Hedonism Series (co-written with J.L. Logosz)

Erotic Excavations (co-written with Clio Evans as Pamela Bones)

Plucked

Visit https://www.valentineverse.com